Text copyright © 1998 by Laurence Anholt. Illustrations copyright © 1998 by Sheila Moxley.
First American edition 1999 published by Orchard Books
First published in Great Britain in 1998 by Doubleday, a division of Transworld Publishers Ltd
Laurence Anholt and Sheila Moxley assert the moral right to be identified as the author and illustrator of this work.
All rights reserved. No part of this book may be reproduced or transmitted in any form or by any means,
electronic or mechanical, including photocopying, recording, or by any information storage or retrieval system,
without permission in writing from the Publisher.

Orchard Books, A Grolier Company, 95 Madison Avenue, New York, NY 10016

Manufactured in Singapore
The text of this book is set in 12 point Weidemann.

1 3 5 7 9 10 8 6 4 2

Library of Congress Cataloging-in-Publication Data
Anholt, Laurence.
Stone girl, bone girl / by Laurence Anholt ; illustrated by Sheila Moxley.
1st American ed.   p. cm.
Summary: A brief biography of the English girl whose discovery of an ichthyosaur skeleton in 1811 when
she was twelve led to a lifelong interest in fossils and other important discoveries.
ISBN 0-531-30148-6 (trade : alk. paper)
1. Anning, Mary, 1799–1847—Juvenile literature. 2. Women paleontologists—England—Biography—
Juvenile literature. [1. Anning, Mary, 1799–1847. 2. Paleontologists. 3. Women—Biography. 4. Fossils.]
I. Moxley, Sheila, ill. II. Title.
QE707.A56A54 1999 560'.92—dc21   98-36608

Stone Girl, Bone Girl

The Story of Mary Anning

by Laurence Anholt
illustrated by Sheila Moxley

Orchard Books   New York

When Mary Anning was a baby, she was struck by lightning. It split a huge elm tree and threw Mary right out of her nurse's arms.

Her father was in his workshop when he heard the terrible news. He dropped his hammer and ran through the stormy streets of Lyme Regis. Gently, he lifted the limp body of his little daughter, and his tears flowed like rain.

But then, an extraordinary thing happened. . . . Mary Anning slowly opened her eyes. She reached out a tiny hand and touched the amazed face of her father. And the little girl began to smile.

It was then her father realized—Mary Anning was no ordinary child.

The years rolled by like waves. Mary grew into a clever girl. "A mind as quick as lightning!" her mother teased.

Mary had few friends, except her father, whom she adored. Like everyone else in the town, she called him "Pepper" because of his speckled beard.

One Saturday, Pepper closed his workshop early. He took Mary down to the cliffs by the crashing sea. She held tightly to his hand because she knew how dangerous it could be. The clay cliffs at Lyme Regis are as soft as melting chocolate. Mary had sometimes seen huge slabs of land slipping and tumbling to the beach below.

Pepper had stories of whole fields on the cliff tops that had disappeared beneath the feet of grazing cattle. He knew a place, he said, where half a farmhouse sat balanced on the cliff edge. He and his quarrymen friends had peered over and seen the remains of the kitchen and even the garden gate, smashed to splinters on the rocks below.

When they came to the place called Black Ven, Pepper reached into his pocket and, to Mary's surprise, took out his best steel hammer. He knelt beside a large rock of dried clay and began carefully tapping away.

"What are you looking for?" asked Mary, dancing about on the sand.

"Just be patient," Pepper said, and laughed.

He worked as if he were making a fine piece of furniture. Mary bent closer. There was something hidden there! Right inside the rock!

At last, Pepper pulled it free and handed the thing to Mary.

"It . . . it's *treasure!*" she gasped.

"It's what we call a little snakestone," Pepper said, smiling. "Just a curiosity. A present for you, Mary."

It was the most beautiful thing Mary had ever seen. Back in the workshop, Pepper polished the snakestone and gave it to Mary to keep.

That night Mary couldn't sleep. Her head swirled
with thoughts like a golden snakestone twisting.
"The cliffs are full of treasure,"
she whispered over and over again.

From that day on, Mary spent every spare moment searching for the curiosities. She had sharp eyes and found them everywhere, in every shape and size—tiny shiny ones, marble ones as big as millstones, others straight as stone fingers or delicate like plants.

Pepper taught her their strange, magical names—thunderbolts, fairy's hearts, crocodile's teeth, devil's toenails. He let Mary have her own special drawer in the workshop for her collection.

But the other children laughed and teased when they saw Mary hunting near the cliffs. Someone made up a rhyme—"Stone Girl, Bone Girl. Out-on-your-own Girl!"—until Mary ran crying to Pepper.

That winter was the wettest and stormiest the town had known.
Great waves smashed the little houses, and the cliffs became softer and
more dangerous still. So Mary stayed away.

The cold, damp air made Pepper feel ill. He looked old and tired,
and sometimes he coughed so loudly that Mary was afraid.

One evening, some rich ladies came to Pepper's workshop. Mary knew who they were—the Philpot sisters, who lived together in a fine house high above the town. "Scientists," people said.

The youngest of the ladies, Annie Philpot, wanted Pepper to build a glass-fronted cabinet. "To display curiosities," she said.

Mary jumped up. She couldn't believe that someone else was interested in curiosities.

"Excuse me," Mary said nervously, "would you like to see my collection?" And she pulled open the drawer.

"Oh!" gasped the ladies. "What wonderful fossils!"

Fossils? Mary had never heard the word. The Misses Philpot smiled. They could see that Mary didn't know much about her collection.

"I'll tell you what, Mary," said Annie Philpot. "When Pepper has finished my little cabinet, why don't you bring it to us? We could have some tea, and then, we will show you our collection."

For three long weeks, she waited for Pepper to finish the cabinet, but he seemed to be working more slowly than ever. Mary was very worried about him.

But at last, the elm cabinet was finished. The wood was from the very same tree that had been struck by lightning and had almost killed baby Mary. She thought it was the most handsome thing that Pepper had ever made.

Slowly, Pepper wrapped the cabinet in brown paper and tied it with string. His old hands were shaking as he kissed Mary.

Mary had never seen anything like the Philpots' house. There were expensive rugs in every room and maids to serve the tea. Most wonderful of all was the collection of curiosities. The Misses Philpot explained that the fossils were the remains of ancient sea creatures that had been preserved in the clay.

Everything was so interesting that Mary forgot to be nervous.
Then, Annie Philpot showed her a huge tooth she had found.

"From a great sea monster," she said. She told Mary she believed
the rest of the creature was still out there, hidden in the cliffs. "If
anyone could ever find that, Mary! That would be the greatest
treasure of all."

It was nearly dark when Mary ran down the hill. As soon as she
pushed open the workshop door, she knew that something was wrong.

The workshop was so quiet after Pepper died. To Mary, it felt like half of her world had fallen away, like the farmhouse on the cliff edge. And there was no money. Her mother began to sell everything she could think of, and still, they went to bed hungry.

One evening, Mary wandered up to the churchyard. A heavy fog hung over everything. Ragged clouds dragged at a lemon-slice moon. As she came to the stone that marked Pepper's grave, something moved in the darkness.

For a moment, Mary was afraid, but coming closer, she realized it was nothing but a funny little dog—a little dog with a coat like speckled pepper!

The dog bounded over and licked Mary's face. When she turned to walk home, the little dog followed her. At last, it ran into the workshop and curled under the table.

"Perhaps you need a friend too," laughed Mary. From that moment, Mary and the dog were never apart.

That summer, the town was full of vacationers.
As Mary and her dog watched the rich ladies and gentlemen wandering the streets, she suddenly had an idea—perhaps she could sell her curiosities!

She dragged a table from the workshop onto the walkway and carefully arranged the fossils from her collection—all except the snakestone around her neck. That she would never part with. She wrote a small sign in her best handwriting: CURIOSITIES FOR SALE. Then, Mary Anning and the little dog sat down to wait.

The first to pass were a group of children. They began laughing and pointing at poor Mary. "Stone Girl, Bone Girl! Out-on-your-own Girl!" they shouted.

All day, Mary waited. She was just about to pack away her table when a group of ladies and gentlemen came by.

"How fascinating!" said a lady.

"What are they?" asked someone else.

"This one would make a delightful brooch. . . ."

"Or a garden ornament . . ."

And so, Mary Anning sold her first fossils—and as the rich people strolled away, Mary felt the weight of coins in her pocket.

"I knew I was right!" she whispered to her dog. "These aren't just ordinary stones—they really are treasures. If only I could find that sea monster!"

CURIOSITIES
FOR SALE

All summer, Mary searched for curiosities for her shop. She borrowed books about fossils from the Misses Philpot and learned everything she could.

Her mother was delighted with the money that Mary was earning, but she was worried about Mary being alone on the dangerous cliffs. Mary reassured her that the little dog would run for help in an emergency.

As she searched, Mary thought more and more about the giant sea monster and about the cliffs in prehistoric times. She imagined fantastic landscapes inhabited by extraordinary creatures.

One morning, Mary was so busy daydreaming, she didn't notice that her dog had wandered away. She ran along the beach, calling for him, but he was nowhere to be seen.

At last, she heard a faint barking, and looking up, she saw the speckled dog high on the sloping side of the cliff.

Mary called for him to come down, but the little dog wouldn't move. He was furiously scratching at something in the clay.

Mary had no choice. She slowly began to climb the rock face. Finally, she reached the little ledge where the dog was standing. Her heart missed a beat. She couldn't believe what she saw. Grinning up at Mary was an enormous skull! The little dog had found the sea monster.

All morning, Mary scraped furiously with Pepper's hammer. There was more than a skull—a whole skeleton, perhaps. But it was far too big for Mary to dig up on her own. Who could help her? Suddenly she remembered Pepper's old friends, the quarrymen.

Leaving the little dog to guard the monster, Mary Anning climbed carefully down to the beach, then ran as fast as she could to the quarry.

"I've found it!" she shouted. "I've found the sea monster!"

In less than ten minutes, Mary was leading a group of quarrymen carrying picks and shovels up the side of the cliff.

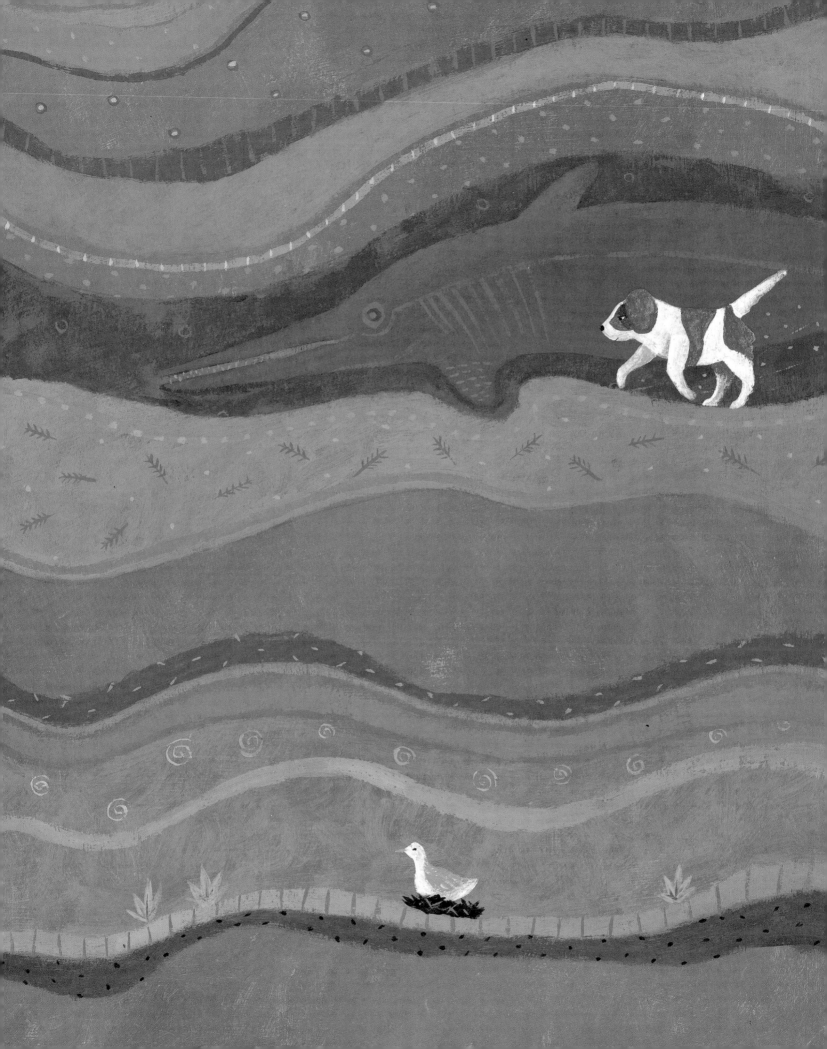

The news spread like fire through the town: "Mary Anning has found the sea monster! Mary Anning has found it!"

An excited crowd gathered on the beach to watch the excavation. The Misses Philpot arrived in their fine clothes and made a tremendous fuss over Mary. Even the children who had teased her came to watch, but they weren't laughing now.

As the evening sun melted into the sea, a strange procession made its way back to the town. A small girl, covered in mud, led the crowd. At the back, six strong quarrymen carefully carried the bones of a real sea monster, as long as a tree and more than one hundred and sixty-five million years old.

The skeleton was laid out on the floor of Pepper's workshop for all the world to see.

For months afterward, visitors came to meet "the Fossil Girl" of Lyme Regis. Famous scientists came in carriages from London, and even the King of Saxony arrived to see for himself.

It was the most important fossil ever found, they said. They called the monster ichthyosaur—"the fish lizard." The museum that bought it paid enough money for Mary and her mother to live happily for the rest of their lives.

But the strange thing was, the little speckled dog had vanished. As if he had done his work and drifted away. Sometimes, Mary imagined she could hear a faint barking from far away in the sea mist. Then, Mary Anning would smile and touch the little snakestone around her neck and step back into the warm workshop, where the shelves were filled with treasures from the dark and dangerous rocks.

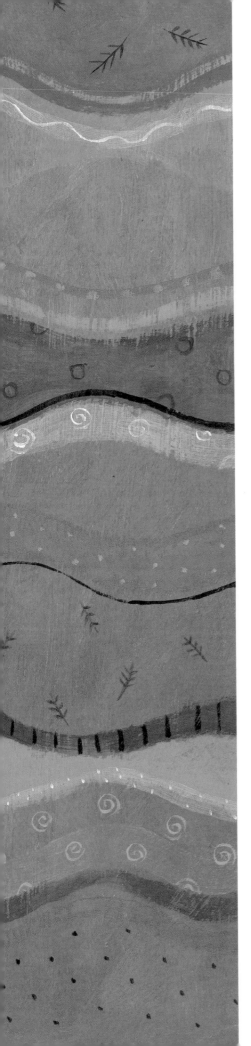
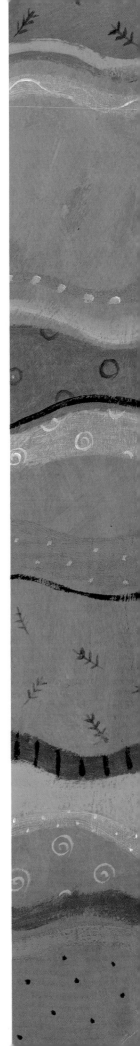

Mary Anning

Mary Anning was born in 1799 and lived all her life in Lyme Regis in Dorset, England. At fifteen months, she survived the lightning strike that killed her nurse and two other girls. Mary was always stubbornly independent, and she became a well-known local character, hunting for fossils accompanied by her little dog. At the time, this was an extraordinary occupation for a young girl.

The great ichthyosaur, which she discovered at the age of twelve, was only the first of Mary's many finds that played an important part in the new science of evolution—eventually leading to Darwin's *On the Origin of Species*, published in 1859. She later uncovered plesiosaurs, pterosaurs, several other ichthyosaurs, and hundreds of other fossils that can still be seen in museums around the world.

Lyme Regis continues to attract fossil hunters, and children still chant the old tongue twister about Mary Anning, the Fossil Girl of Lyme Regis. . . .

She sells seashells by the seashore.
The shells she sells are seashells I'm sure.
So, if she sells seashells by the seashore,
I'm sure the shells are seashore shells.

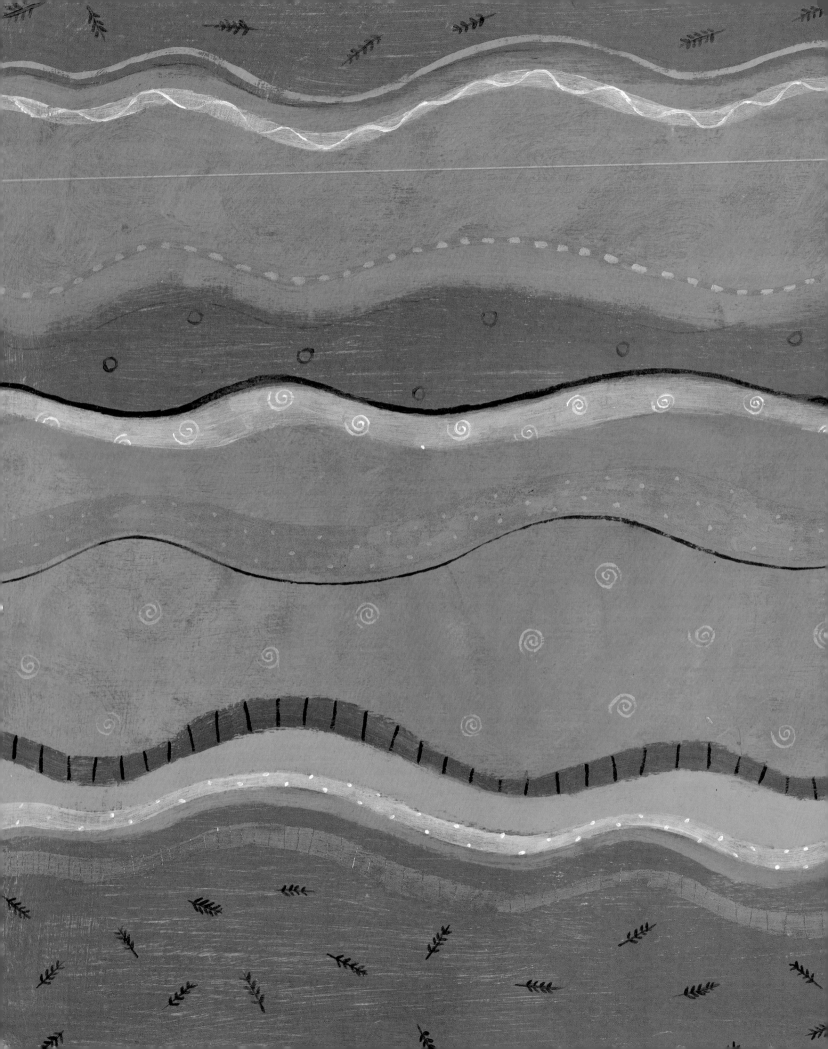